D0004403

Firefly Friend

by **Kimberly Wagner Klier**
Illustrated by Michael Garland

New Hanover County Public
201 Chestnut Stre
Wilmington, NC

For my mother, Mary Byrd
—K.W.K.

To Peggy
—M.G.

Reading Consultants
Linda Cornwell
Literacy Specialist

Katharine A. Kane
Education Consultant
(Retired, San Diego County Office of Education and San Diego State University)

Library of Congress Cataloging-in-Publication Data
Klier, Kimberly.
  Firefly friend / written by Kimberly Wagner Klier ; illustrated by Michael Garland.
    p. cm. — (A Rookie reader)
  Summary: A child follows a firefly in the night, wondering what it is trying to say.
  ISBN 0-516-25895-8 (lib. bdg.)   0-516-26817-1 (pbk.)
  [1. Fireflies—Fiction. 2. Stories in rhyme.] I. Garland, Michael, 1952- ill. II. Title. III. Series.
  PZ8.3.K.6797Fi 2004
  [E]–dc22
                              2003018654

CHILDREN'S PRESS, and A ROOKIE READER®, and associated logos are trademarks and or
registered trademarks of Scholastic Library Publishing. SCHOLASTIC and
associated logos are trademarks and or registered trademarks of Scholastic Inc.
1 2 3 4 5 6 7 8 9 10 R 13 12 11 10 09 08 07 06 05 04

Firefly friend comes out to play when the sun is tucked away.

His light blinks far across the lawn.

His light blinks off.
His light blinks on.

His light blinks high
in the apple tree.

His light blinks off.
Where can he be?

His little light blinks a bright "hello."

His light blinks off.
Where did he go?

His light blinks on beside my ear.

What does he say? I try to hear.

Does he wish me a happy night?

He blinks at me. I think he might.

His light blinks out across the lawn.

It's time for bed. I start to yawn.

I'll sleep for now,
but tomorrow night,

I'll look again for firefly light.

Word List (63 words)

a	ear	it's	start
across	far	lawn	sun
again	firefly	light	the
apple	for	little	think
at	friend	look	time
away	go	me	to
be	happy	might	tomorrow
bed	he	my	tree
beside	hear	night	try
blinks	hello	now	tucked
bright	high	off	what
but	his	on	when
can	I	out	where
comes	I'll	play	wish
did	in	say	yawn
does	is	sleep	

About the Author

Kimberly Wagner Klier is an author and grade school teacher. She lives in Indiana with her husband Tim. They raise Appaloosa horses and two dogs, Brownie and Max.

About the Illustrator

Michael Garland lives in Patterson, New York. Besides illustrating, Michael enjoys writing and has penned many children's books and articles for *American Artist* Magazine.